DISSEVERMENT

Z.C. KROL

Cover designed by Taylor Kerns

This is for my buddy Nate, who, upon hearing
my idea for this, said: *"Haha, I hate this so much.
This is so cursed. Please write this."*

Welp, I wrote it.

- Z

DISSEVERMENT

SECTION ONE

I never thought I'd have contact with my mother again, until a letter arrived for me in June of 2009. I was twenty-nine at the time, living in a small house with my then-fiancée Madelyn. She was the one who brought it inside with a concerned look on her face, a face that was usually so reassuring. I know now that she had a feeling — not a concrete image, but an abstract sense of danger in the white envelope. She was never the type to get feelings or premonitions of dread, but the moment has since made me question the supernatural, and whether she has a sensitivity for it.

"What's that, Little Dipper?" I asked her after a sip from my beer. Her look of alarm suggested they were test results saying I had six weeks to live, though the flap on the back of the envelope remained glued down, so she had no way of knowing that. I was confident I had a few decades left (the beer probably wasn't helping).

"You got a letter, Big Dipper," she answered simply. She seemed hesitant to make the transfer of it from her hand to mine, keeping it flat and secure against her chest.

"From who?"

"Doesn't have a return address."

After she finally handed it over, I took out the folded piece of paper and opened it to discover a typed note addressed to me.

Hello Tyler, it began.

Two things happened after that. The first was that I memorized the letter, all 140 words of it. I read it over and over again, studying each line, each character rendered in 12-point serif font (Times New Roman, if I'm not mistaken). The second thing was that my nightmares — ones I hadn't had since before meeting Madelyn — returned. Nightmares about shouting, and surgical knives, and bile.

This was a Friday evening, and I decided, against my instincts, to call my father before I went to sleep, before the first nightmare started again. I asked him if we could meet for breakfast that next morning. He was surprised to hear from me, and asked what the unexpected reunion was about. I didn't tell him. In retrospect, I think he knew.

Maddy insisted on going to the restaurant with me, but I forbade her. I had never told her the dark details of my past; just the easy, comfortable version. I didn't think she would've been able to grasp all of it. It was too much. She would've thought differently of me. She had heard enough to be sympathetic and supportive, but I could never allow disgust to invade her affection for me. She had never met my father, nor my mother, and I wasn't about to drag her into my mess before our wedding that October.

This is unfortunately not the most appropriate way to introduce myself to you.

I arrived at Sunny's for breakfast promptly at 7:30 AM, a time I rarely saw on Saturdays anymore, much less after so little sleep. In my delirium, I was stunned to see that my father had arrived at the restaurant before me: alone in a booth, facing me, elbows on the table, hands clasped together in front of his face as if in prayer (though he most certainly was not). The reality that he showed up anywhere for me, let alone early, was a foreign concept I quickly had to shake off.

I sat across from him. I felt my face burning and wondered if he could tell. There were a few seconds of silence. We didn't say hello.

"Still with that Black girl?" he asked.

That girl. That Black girl. The nerve. The woman I'd been with for ten years. "Madelyn," I said shakily.

"Yeah. Me and Maddy are engaged. Getting married in October."

He scoffed. "You're not here to invite me to the wedding, and you certainly didn't wanna get breakfast."

I took a beat. I didn't want to tell him he was right, but he was.

But circumstances give me no other choice.

"Mom's sick," I said.

We stared into each other's eyes. He looked older. Of course he did.

A young waitress approached our table with cosmic timing. "Hello fellas, my name is Emma and I will be taking care of you this morning. Can I start you guys off with any drinks?" She looked at him first.

"Coffee. Regular. *Black*," he said.

"Same," I said.

"Alright, and then did you guys want to order now or are you still looking at the menus?"

"Still looking," I answered. "We just need a few minutes."

I looked at her and she looked at me, and although I couldn't tell her telepathically that this breakfast meeting was about more than just breakfast, I think she got the message from my pleading eyes.

"Alright," she said cheerfully in her best waitress voice, "I'll be back in a little bit with your coffee and I'll see if you're ready to order, okay?"

We nodded. She walked away.

My father picked up his menu and opened it, scanning the pages.

"Sick with what?" he finally asked.

My name is Kenneth Shepherd, and I am your stepfather.

"Got a letter in the mail from her husband," I answered. "Turns out I have a stepdad. How 'bout that?"

He set his menu down. "Sick with *what?*" he asked again, irritated.

"She's dying," I said. "She wants to see me. There isn't much time."

I married your mother Donna less than a year ago.

We sat for another minute in silence. Emma returned with immaculate timing and a pot of coffee, and filled our cups. "I'll... give you a few more minutes, okay?"

I nodded. My father ignored her. She moved on to her next table. I picked up my menu this time. I didn't know what else to do, where else to go — literally or figuratively.

There is no better way to say this, so please forgive my bluntness.

He finally let out a loud sigh. Not an exaggerated sigh, not a fake, dramatic sigh for attention, but a genuine exhalation of what may have been sorrow.

"Tyler, I was never the best father, alright?" he began. "I don't have to tell you that. If I could go back and do everything differently, I would. But I can't. But I do know one thing I was good at, the *one* thing, probably, and that was being honest with you. I never lied to her or to you. You know why I left. You know why I couldn't handle it anymore."

Your mother is very ill and does not have much time left.

This might've been the most honest I'd ever seen him, contrary to the sentiment he'd just expressed, and it was maybe the most words he'd said to me at once in years. If I didn't know what to do before, I was really at a loss now.

"What's this have to do with anything?" I asked. I was almost in shock, I think. My father was a characteristically quiet man, regardless of how long it'd been since we last spoke. I hadn't heard this much sincerity tumble from his mouth since he left my mother years earlier.

"Don't go see her," he implored.

"What? She's dying, Dad." I surprised even myself by the title I gave him. He looked surprised, too. I didn't choose to call him Dad; it just happened. I couldn't have imagined calling him Ray or Raymond. He was neither at that moment. He was Dad.

She really wants to see you, Tyler, one last time before she's gone.

I wondered. It was a weird and macabre way to bring my father and myself back together, back to a hint of closeness, but maybe the inevitable demise of my mother was exactly the catalyst we both needed.

"Tyler, trust me," he said. "Nothing good can come of it. Nothing ever good came from being near her."

"She's dying," I said again, feeling the weight of my sleepless night.

"Dying from what?" he asked. The smirk on his face suggested he wasn't buying anything the letter was attempting to sell, before he'd even read it. And that was when I pulled the letter out of my pocket and set it on the table. It was still in the envelope, the flap now detached. He reached across and grabbed it, took it out, but didn't begin reading it yet.

Please reach me at the number below and we can discuss meeting arrangements and directions.

"Kenneth didn't say in the letter. Just that she's sick."

"Kenneth is his name? Her — your stepdad?" There was maybe a bit of pain in his voice at the word. Maybe just awkwardness.

"Yes," I answered.

"Nobody in their right mind would've married her if they knew, Tyler. You know her."

"Maybe she changed before she got sick. Maybe he helped her."

"It had already gone too far," my father said. "There was no going back from that. You saw it. And you made a decision for yourself. The correct one."

"Maybe."

He turned his eyes to the letter and began reading it. I watched him, I anticipated each word I had memorized before I saw his eyes move to it. I watched his face with each sentence he passed, trying to see microexpressions.

"Shepherd, huh," he said. My stepfather's last name. "I can have someone at the station look him up."

I shook my head before he'd finished his thought. "I don't want to start something."

"Nobody has to know. You won't be 'starting' anything."

"I'm sure he's fine," I reasoned. But the truth was, I wasn't sure if Kenneth Shepherd was "fine." I had never heard of him. He had dropped into my universe without warning.

I know you have not been on speaking terms with your mother.

"No return address," my father said. Now he was acting like *Raymond Swanson, Sergeant Detective* and not *Ray Swanson, Father of Tyler Swanson*. Or maybe it was the other way around. "Didn't write the note by hand, went out of his way to type it on a computer and print it. Didn't write it on a piece of notebook paper? So official, isn't it? Is he a judge?"

He wasn't wrong; it was odd. And it didn't take a detective to see that. "You're reaching," I said, trying not to agree. "Maybe he prefers typing. Maybe he has sloppy handwriting. Maybe he didn't know if he was sending the letter to the right Tyler Swanson. Maybe he sent it to a hundred Tyler Swansons and he didn't want all of them to have his address or have his handwriting."

And it's unfair to shock you with the news of having a stepfather like this.

My father snickered. "You could look up 'Kenneth Shepherd' easily. And you could find the announcement of his marriage to your mother. And you could find his address. It's public record."

"Just finish the letter, would you?"

With each word he finished, he looked more and more annoyed, bordering on angry, almost as if he was becoming protective of me. Another foreign feeling.

But considering the circumstances, please make the effort to fulfill one of your mom's final wishes.

"You don't owe this guy a fucking thing. And you don't owe her anything either. 'Make the effort' my ass. Is she so sick that she couldn't call you or send this letter herself? Doubt it."

"What am I supposed to do?" I asked. "Do I just ignore this?"

"Yes," my father said. "I'm telling you, Ty, don't bother. You don't need to see her."

"I bothered calling *you*," I snapped. "I bothered wanting to see *you*. I didn't have to see *you*, either." I immediately regretted saying this, and I regretted the way my voice was getting bigger. I was sure the booth next to us heard me.

"I'm not a crazy fucking bitch like your mom," my father snapped back quietly, leaning in close.

"A crazy fucking bitch that you *left* me with," I said with a bigger, shakier voice, also leaning in.

Sincerely,

Kenneth

We both stopped. We knew we were in public. We knew that escalating this any further would cause a scene and someone would intervene. We knew. So we stopped. We sat in silence, we let our nerves settle, and we tried again.

"I'm going, Dad. Do you want to come with me?"

He considered it calmly.

"This is not my fight, Ty. Not anymore. I walked away from it. A long time ago. I told you. I regret leaving you, I wish with all my heart that I had been strong enough to take you with me, but I was exhausted. I didn't leave you in danger, I didn't purposely make you a prisoner to her, I just walked away. I ran. I didn't think. I didn't think I was leaving you *with* that. I was just leaving, period."

The waitress, Emma, came back, and this time she wasn't her fake, cheery self. I knew she felt the tension at our booth, saw the tired looks on our faces from argument, from digging up old memories, scratching at healing wounds. "Are you gentlemen ready to order?"

My father and I looked at each other, and for just a moment, we were two normal people. Father and son getting breakfast on a Saturday morning, with no problems, who were just hungry and wanted pancakes.

"I think so," I said. And I did something I didn't think I would do when I walked into that restaurant: I smiled. And my father smiled, too. The honesty felt good. Letting out the rage, those feelings, after so much time, felt good.

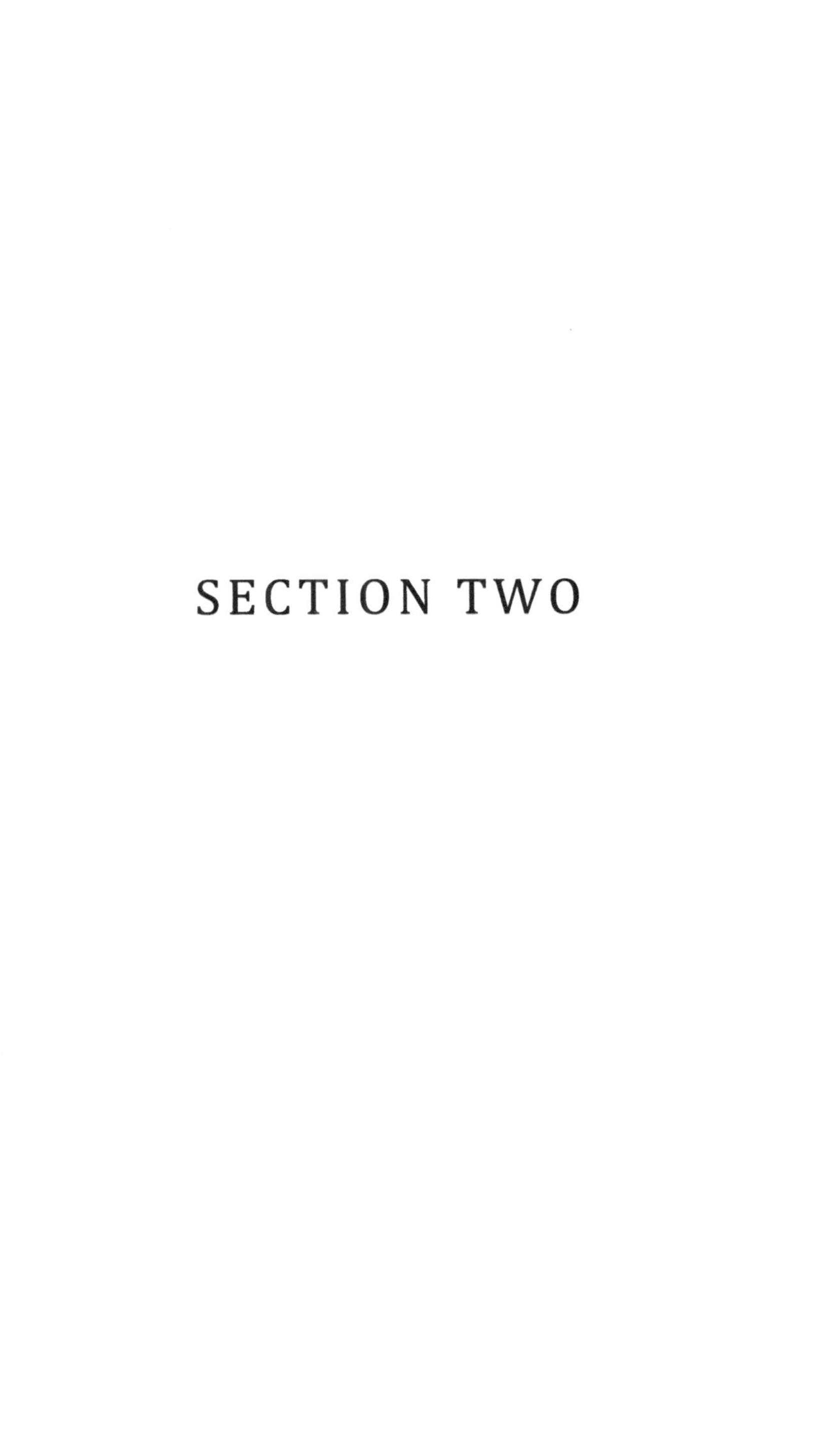

SECTION TWO

I decided to tell Maddy everything when I got home. I don't know why. I don't know why I wanted her to know all the pain of my childhood. Maybe it was because I had made a breakthrough with my father, a step towards a possible relationship with him, or maybe it was because I had barely slept the night before. All I know is that when I opened my front door and walked into my house, my fiancée was standing there, and she was too damn smart to believe any lie I could've told her.

"You've been crying," she said, heartbroken.

I smiled. My dry, red eyes were impossible to hide, and I wasn't the sunglasses type. I didn't even own a pair. "I was. In my car. On the drive home."

"What did he say to you? What did he do?"

"It actually went surprisingly well," I said. "I'm not really upset or angry. I'm just exhausted. And relieved. And confused, I guess. It went well, I promise. I'm okay."

"Did you eat?"

"I did. We both did. I wasn't expecting either of us would stick around for that, but we did. That's why I've been crying, their sausage links were terrible. Way too greasy."

Maddy smiled. "Not everything has to be a joke, you know." She walked quickly to me and wrapped her arms around me, planting her chin on my shoulder. I took in her embrace, the smell of her hair, and then a long exhale finally escaped as I closed my eyes.

"I think it's time to tell you some things you don't know," I whispered into her ear. That sentence alone took a lot for me to say to her. Suddenly, there was confirmation. There was officially more to my story. There was more to the guy Madelyn Strong thought she knew intimately.

She raised her head and her eyes locked onto mine. "If you're ready," she said back. I could see in her expression that she had been waiting patiently for this moment, that she knew there was more to the simple yarn I spun for her about my life before we fell in love.

She led me to the couch and told me to rest. She went to the kitchen and soon came back with a bottle of beer and a glass of wine. It was ten in the morning and neither of us cared. Screw it.

I took a long drink and rested the bottle on one knee. She placed one of her hands on my other knee. I pulled the letter out of my pants pocket and said, "This letter, from Kenneth, it says my mom's sick." Maddy nodded. She knew this; I had shown her the letter the night before. "But she was always sick, Madelyn. She always had an illness slowly taking her life."

I continued with the earliest memory I had of my mother's affliction, when I was eight. My father told me to go upstairs and wait in my bedroom while he and Mommy talked. I didn't last long on my bed before I snuck out and crept to the top of the steps, trying so hard not to make a creak on the wooden floor. And I sat on the top step while they yelled at each other.

"I love you the way you are, Donna," he had said. *"You look fine. There's nothing wrong with you."*

"How can you love me? Look at me."

"What about you? You're fine. You're the woman I married. You're the mother of my child. I'll always love you."

"I'm a fat fucking cow."

"You knock it off," he yelled. *"You heard the doctor. You heard both doctors. You're unhealthy. You're ninety-eight fucking pounds, Donna. You need to cut this shit out."*

"I'm obese, Raymond. Clinically obese. Morbidly obese. Why can't you see it? Every mirror in this house makes me fucking sick. Are you blind?"

"You are not obese. They explained this to you. They showed you the scale. Multiple scales. Charts."

"Those things are not accurate."

"You need to eat, god damn it. You're getting weak. You fell down at work. You could die. Is that what you want? Do you want to miss Tyler growing up?"

"What I want is to not be a fucking whale. And you won't support me."

"Donna, you have no more weight to lose, baby. You're reaching a dangerous point where you'll cause serious problems that you can't recover from. Sweetheart, you could die."

I could tell Madelyn suddenly didn't know what she had gotten herself into, falling in love with me, deciding to become my wife. She knew this was just the beginning of a tale cutting much deeper. And she was right.

"It started with the starving," I said calmly. "Then it got a little more extreme. I remember hearing her whisper to herself while standing on the bathroom scale, 'Every ounce counts,' and then it really took off from there."

"Bulimia?" Maddy guessed.

"Mutilation."

Maddy squeezed my knee.

I could hear my mother saying it in my head. *Every ounce counts. Every ounce counts.* I'd think it to myself until the rhyming of the words made the whole phrase nonsensical and silly. *Ounts-counts. Ounts-counts.*

"It was subtle at first, so my dad wouldn't find out. He didn't know for almost a year. They never touched each other anymore. Not even a kiss goodbye before work. But I could tell, sitting close to her, she was in pain under her clothes. She ached or had to move in certain ways that didn't seem natural. To avoid pain."

"What did she do?" Maddy asked. Something about her now, the childishness of her voice and eyes, I could tell she was scared. She was never scared; I'd made sure of it since we started dating. I promised myself no one I loved would ever live in fear like I did, and yet, here she was, alien to me.

The irony of Maddy's last name, Strong, was never lost on me. I was attracted to her *because* she was strong, unlike my mother — that lost, miserable, frail woman who brought me into the world. Madelyn was successful: a self-made woman who started her own fitness studio in town, whose goal was to live a life of good health and to help others become healthier and stronger. Her business, unashamedly called Mad Strong Fitness, was the most popular exercise studio in our county, and it wasn't hard to see why. Maddy was the head coach and individually helped each client who attended. It wasn't just a business for her. It was a mission. And I loved her even more for it. They all called her "Mad" for short and she loved it, but that was a name I never used. She was just my Maddy. She was also Little Dipper, because the smattering of little moles on her right inner thigh looked like the constellation. I, of course, became Big Dipper because of my nickname for her.

But right now, Mad Strong was anything but, and I didn't know if I could keep telling her what had happened next. I started slow.

"She would make herself vomit. Little excuses here and there like a meal didn't settle right, or she caught a bug. I was little but I wasn't stupid. And my dad certainly wasn't. He dragged her out of the house and into the car to take her to a crisis center. She screamed and said she'd tell them he was abusing her, that they'd take me away from him, that he'd never see me again. And then he'd turn the car around, he'd give up, and that was that. Until it wasn't just that anymore."

Maddy didn't blink once when I said this. "Didn't you... you think about calling the police? Or telling a teacher at school?" she asked.

"My dad *was* the police," I tried to explain. "And a bunch of his colleagues would know. It would've killed him. Plus, she was doing it to herself. My dad kept telling me it was her choice and there was no helping it. If she wanted to die, no doctor was going to convince her otherwise. He just got numb to the whole thing. He stopped caring. He was seeing much more terrible things at work."

"Did you or your dad think she *wanted* to die?"

"I didn't think she was trying to kill herself. She wanted to look different. 'Better.' What her eyes were seeing in the mirror wasn't what her brain was registering."

"Sure," Maddy agreed. "Body dysmorphia. Leads to depression and anxiety. Leads to eating disorders. I've seen plenty of it at the studio. Girl wants to 'work' on her thighs and I just want to tell her she looks like a damn supermodel compared to others there. I'd never say that, of course."

I took another long drink of the beer she had brought me. "It gets worse," I said.

Madelyn adjusted herself on the couch, sat up straighter to prepare, and I continued.

"She would find these doctors online — well, I wouldn't call them *doctors;* I don't know what the hell they were — and I remember my dad calling them and threatening them. She would find them in underground places, unofficial places. I don't know how to explain it. They were illegal operations. Back-alley butchers. That's what my dad called them."

"Jesus Christ," Maddy said.

Every ounce counts, I thought.

"It started reasonably, if reasonable is the right word. She decided she didn't want to have any more children. That was the reason for her hysterectomy. Then she decided she was having bad stomach cramps and needed her gallbladder removed. No real doctor would've gone along with it with zero tests and no evidence of gallstones. No ultrasounds or X-rays."

Every ounce counts.

"She read up on this stuff. She knew what was essential. She knew what was just enough to keep her alive. Suddenly she discovered she only needed one kidney. That was after her appendix was taken out. That was after she said her tonsils were enlarged and there was a risk of her breathing being cut off."

Every ounce counts.

"Then there were parts I'd never even heard of before. The palmaris longus, a muscle that apparently helps flex the wrist. A decent chunk of the world's population is born without it. Not essential. No big deal."

"And your dad did nothing? You were just stuck watching her... wither?"

"He kept himself busy," I said. "Hours are tough for cops, especially junior detectives, which he had just been promoted to at the time."

"How long did this go on for?" Maddy asked.

I snickered. "It's all I remember. My dad finally left when I was thirteen. He knew I could take care of myself until I turned eighteen, and he knew she would never hurt me. She wasn't abusing *me* or anything. She never hit me."

"But it *was* abuse," Madelyn argued. "She was exposing her mental illness to you. For a child to see that behavior and that mentality, it's amazing you turned out alright."

I took another sip. "I did?"

Maddy smiled meekly, then: "What made you stop talking to her?"

"I ran away."

"Literally?"

I nodded. "After I turned eighteen, I just took off and never looked back. I never said goodbye to her. I went to my high school graduation by myself, said goodbye to a couple of friends, and I just got out. I decided a few weeks after the accident in the kitchen."

She didn't respond.

"She 'accidentally' cut off a finger while making dinner," I said with air quotes. "She thought it was hysterical. 'What a clutz,' she said, and she promised she was alright. But I knew. I knew that would be the first of eight fingers and two thumbs. And eventually toes."

Every ounce counts.

Madelyn cupped her hands over one of mine.

"And I wasn't going to stick around and watch. Just like my father," I continued. "And you know, I really don't blame him. I can't hate him. I don't know what I can feel towards him. It's always been a challenge to sort of understand *what* I feel about him. Some days I wish he would've just scooped me up and got me out of there, picked me up in his police car, hit the lights, and off we go."

"He should've," Maddy said. "That son of a bitch."

I shrugged. "People handle things in different ways. Some deny it's happening, or they ignore it."

"But to ignore the environment your child is growing up in..."

"Yeah," I said, cutting her off. "I think about it all the time. Or at least I did."

"What do you mean?" she said.

"Maddy, when I met you, when I walked into your studio wanting to lose a few pounds, and I realized who you were, not just outside — which is very lovely I might add — but inside too, I knew I could put all this bullshit behind me and just be at peace. Until this goddamn letter."

She considered what I'd said and was clearly flattered, but there was more on her mind. She thought about it for a moment, then formed the words. "Big Dipper, you were never at peace with this. You distracted yourself. I was a distraction to you, no matter how good of a distraction I've been. I think this letter was a good thing. This is a blessing. You have a chance to *actually* make peace with it. You never said goodbye, and now you can. And it'll be the *only* time you can. You can't deny yourself that opportunity. We're getting married in a few months and we're starting a new life together. Our life. Let's start it off on the right foot, you know? This is a positive thing, baby. Closure."

Of course, I knew she was right, as much as I didn't want to admit it.

I kissed her on the lips, lingering and grateful. "Thank you," I said.

"Thank you for telling me," she replied. "I'm so proud of you and I'm happy you told me. I had a bad feeling when I brought the letter inside, but I was wrong."

I nodded. I looked at the letter in my lap and remembered there was a phone number at the bottom.

SECTION THREE

I paced back and forth in my house later that day with my cell in my hand. Maddy was coaching classes at her studio, I was by myself, and the number was dialed; all I had to do was tap the green phone icon.

I had a stepfather all of a sudden. I hadn't taken the time to really let that sink in, since my mind was preoccupied with the nightmares of shouting, of surgical knives, and bile, with all the memories of my youth and telling my fiancée all of it, with seeing my father again — it was a lot to take in. Too much. But I kept repeating to myself what Maddy had so eloquently told me: *This is a positive thing. This is closure. This is getting things on the right foot.*

I called the number. It rang three times.

"Hello?" a man's voice answered. The simple, single word had a husky quality, not intimidating, but authoritative. Not necessarily pleasant. Busy. Bothered.

I froze. I just stood in the living room with the phone against my ear.

"Hello," the voice said again, this time not a question seeking a response. Irritated.

I faked a cough of acknowledgment that I was there, then held my breath. "Hi, uh, hello? I got this — letter — in the mail, and..."

"Tyler?" the man suddenly interrupted.

"Yes," I said.

"Tyler Swanson?"

"Yes. Kenneth?"

"Oh my god," he said, his rough voice suddenly getting higher, "it's so nice to hear from you, Tyler. Yes, it's Kenneth."

I didn't respond. I froze again, having no idea what the hell to say.

Kenneth broke the silence. "I'm so glad you called."

"Yeah, well," I managed dumbly.

"I know it was weird just sending you a letter like that. I just — there were a few Tyler Swansons in the state and I had no idea where to begin. And frankly, I was just so nervous about talking to you, I had no idea how to reach out, or if you were even the right guy. I'm sorry if I was cryptic or strange. You probably thought it was the weirdest damn thing."

I could tell he was excited and relieved. He spoke quickly, like he was taken aback, not expecting this call. I instantly had a different impression of him.

"It was unusual, yeah," I said. "But I... No worries."

"I was just conflicted about sending out too much information to a stranger if it wasn't you."

"It's really no problem," I insisted. I walked over to the couch and sat down, deciding that this was turning out okay and I could finally try to relax.

"Listen, Tyler. It's all true, what I said. And I'm sorry to have to break awful news like that in a letter. It's not fair, man. Donna just — your mom just really begged and pleaded for me to find you."

"Well, I'm glad you found me," I said, and that was honest. "She's sick, then?"

"Yeah. Yes. Cancer. Stage four. I'm so sorry."

A punch in the gut. This was not the "illness" I was expecting. Deep down I thought my father could've been right at the restaurant, with his smirk and his persistence in my not contacting her. I just wouldn't admit it to myself. Suddenly this was very real, even more real than something of her own doing. I wanted to call my father and tell him, *Fuck you, she really is dying. How dare you grin and sit there with your fucking smug look on your face. 'You still dating that Black girl?' Eat shit.*

"So, cancer. That's it?" I asked.

Kenneth was silent for a moment, then replied, "I'm sorry, what do you mean?"

"She's just sick with cancer?"

"I'm afraid I'm confused, Tyler."

I tried again with another fake cough. "How... is she otherwise?"

"Oh, Tyler," Kenneth said like he had had an epiphany. "I know what you mean now. Wow. It's been so long, I forgot."

"Forgot?"

"Tyler, me and your mother have been together for about eight years now. Got married last year, and well, yeah, she had an eating disorder and... other emotional issues then, but we worked on it, early on, and she recovered."

She *recovered?* The word rang in my mind.

"She's put all that behind her. She's really better now. I'd like to think I had a part in that. I tried my best to help her, and she was doing great, except, you know, then the cancer came."

"I don't know what to say. I wasn't quite... prepared for this." The image of her finger on the kitchen floor as she laughed. She *recovered.*

"She wants to see you, man. One last time. Or maybe it could even be a couple times. Whatever you want. And I'd love to meet you, too. I know this is a tall order, but she really wanted me to find you."

"This is a lot to process," I reiterated. "I really didn't think she would recover from... that."

"Believe me, I completely understand. I'm sure you've moved on with life and this was the last thing you wanted, and now to hear that she doesn't have much longer, with something else..."

"Right."

"Listen," Kenneth said, "I found your address, obviously, and I noticed you're about two hours away from us. Can I give you my address? Do you have a pen and paper?"

"Kenneth... Mr. Shepherd, I..."

"Tyler, please, call me Ken."

"Ken, I just... I'm not sure I can do this. Or if I want to."

"I know. Listen, I'll give you the address, you can decide if you want to come up or not. Just shoot me a text and I'll be ready, okay? We have no plans tomorrow or next weekend. But please keep in mind there's not much time left. This is really, really important to her."

"Okay," I answered.

"Okay?" Kenneth asked, confirming.

"Yeah."

"You got a pen and paper?"

I answered yes and grabbed a pen off the side table next to me, and prepared to write the address on the palm of my free hand. I tucked the phone between my ear and shoulder while I got the information.

"Tyler, real quick," Kenneth added after. "Thanks so much for calling, man. I really appreciate it. Please call or text any time."

We exchanged farewells and I hung up. I sat on the couch in silence for well over an hour, meditating over the weekend so far. In less than twenty-four hours, life-altering information just dropped onto my lap like an atom bomb. I was nervous. I was scared. I had an anxiety I hadn't felt in longer than a decade. I thought that pit in my stomach, those rancid butterflies flying around in the cage of my center were gone. But here they were again, flapping their rotted wings, spitting cortisol like dragons breathe fire. She *recovered.*

I lost track of time, adrift in my worries, until Madelyn walked through the front door. She was still in her coaching outfit, looking tired and beautiful, glistening from time on an exercise bike or a treadmill or both. She took pride in performing every workout along with her clients, but sometimes, after so many classes in a day, she would need to just stand and observe. Today she had clearly joined them.

She stood near the entrance of the living room, her gym bag strapped over her shoulder. "Hey," she said, and paused. Probably because of the look on my face I hadn't realized I was wearing. "You alright?"

"I called him," I said.

"Kenneth?" She knew that's what I meant but she asked anyway.

I nodded.

"Oh my God, baby," she said, putting her gym bag on the floor and walking over to the couch. "I'm so proud of you. How'd it go?" She hovered over me, not wanting to sit down in her sweaty clothes.

"Bittersweet," I said. "She has cancer. Advanced. He told me that all the other shit? From back in the day? She overcame it. He helped her with therapy and recovery, I guess. That part's all over."

"Wow, that's good to hear. I mean, considering — everything else. How do you feel, honey? Are you okay?"

"I don't know."

"Talk to me," she said.

I wasn't quite on the verge of crying. I'd already cried that morning after leaving the restaurant. I wasn't sure if I was numb now, or still ruminating on what I was told. "I feel like there's so much time lost that didn't need to be. And now there's no getting it back, you know?"

"But you at least have this chance to see her, right? And all of that from before, that's over with. You don't have to worry about seeing that again."

"Right."

She leaned down and kissed me on my forehead. "I'm proud of you, Big Dipper. And I'm also in desperate need of a shower. I'm disgusting. I'll get dinner started as soon as I'm out, okay? And we can talk more."

I nodded again. I watched her walk up the stairs, and another wave of adrenaline washed up my gut and into my chest. Two more surges crashed through in the span of maybe five minutes, and I whispered to myself, "It's okay. Everything's okay." But of course, saying that was also admitting something was wrong, and I was compounding the cycles into a worse wrong. The paradox of dread.

I got up and paced around the room, unsure of what to do. I didn't think it was a panic attack or anything worse, but I walked up the stairs anyway, needing Madelyn. I walked slowly into the steamy bathroom so I wouldn't startle her.

"Honey?" I said softly, but she didn't hear me under the rain of shower water. "Little Dipper?" I said louder.

She finally opened the shower curtain. What was standing in front of me was a work of art and still the most beautiful woman I'd ever seen. Her dark skin was wet and gorgeous.

"Baby?" she said.

I broke down into tears. I had no idea where it came from. It just happened. My face became almost as drenched as hers. "I'm scared."

She turned the shower off and stepped out of the tub, and wrapped her arms around me, getting my clothes wet. "Baby, it's okay. It's okay."

"I don't know what to do," I said.

She squeezed me tight. "You don't have to go. You do whatever you want, okay? I'm right here. I'm always here. You do whatever you need. I'm here."

I sobbed into her shoulder and she kissed my hair and my cheeks, and eventually my lips. "I love you so much," I said. I could smell her body wash and shampoo and her hair — her air — was intoxicating, her skin warm from the hot shower.

She let go to reach for a towel, her back now to me, and I couldn't resist touching her and binding my arms around her waist. I kissed the back of her neck while my hands slowly reached up to the undersides of her breasts. The disarray of my emotions converted into a different energy, and she welcomed it with the same energy.

We cherished each other that afternoon and into the night, embracing and swaying to the cadence of what was only love, her body fluttering and sending better waves of excitement through my body, better forces flying around the cage of my center. I felt at home and free from harm, and it didn't matter anymore what I decided. I was invincible with her devotion, and as we lay in bed later in our calm euphoria, I told her I was going to drive to the address tomorrow. I was going alone, and I was going to put it all behind me for good. She stared into my eyes with pride and we fell asleep in each other's arms with no interest in dinner, floating, weightless.

The next morning, I walked downstairs and into the kitchen where Maddy had the room filled with the amazing aromas of breakfast staples. She looked at me and smiled Good Morning. "Last night was..." she began.

"Amazing," I finished.

"Too simple of a word." She smiled again. "I might need you stressed and scared more often."

I could see a slight regret on her face after saying that, and I had to assure her that it was okay. "You're the best distraction. You keep me stable."

"Well, my legs were barely stable this morning," she joked.

I pinched her bottom and she squealed in surprise. I laughed. "Glad I can still turn you into jelly."

I told her I'd be gone most of the day, and it was convenient since she had a twelve-hour shift at the studio. I told her I had texted Kenneth and he was more than thrilled for me to drive there later in the morning. She expressed again how proud of me she was and that she was excited that I was closing this chapter in a very long story that would end happily with us.

"I'm making eggs and bacon and toast," she said a few moments later, still standing over the stove. "Want anything else?"

"I might need *you* again before I leave."

"I'm part of a complete breakfast," she said with a smirk.

Looking back at that moment, I remember how happy she always made me — and still does — and how even though I thought I was a complete person back then, it was more important that she made me *feel* like a complete person — and always did.

SECTION FOUR

Every ounce counts, I thought as I pulled over and threw up eggs and bacon and toast on rough pavement. I was a little more than halfway to Kenneth Shepherd's address and considered turning around, back to Maddy, where I knew it was safe.

But it wasn't just about safety. It was about this moment, this puddle from my gut maybe six feet from the dead possum I now noticed, red innards tarnishing roadway.

This anxiety, these attacks, this grease in my throat, would never go away if I turned back in cowardice. Maddy told me I didn't have to go, but I knew she would be disappointed in me if I didn't. And I knew I'd never forgive myself.

I coughed a few times, trying not to look at the carcass, and leaned back up into my car and shut the door. I grabbed my phone. I'm doing this, I thought. I'm not turning around. And I'm letting him know.

I called my father. Thankfully, it went to voicemail. "Hey, uh," I started, then wiped a bit of disgorge from my bottom lip. "I know you said not to go, but I'm going. On my own. I'm glad you and I made some sense of peace. It felt good. I don't know if that leads to anything or where we go next, but I gotta make peace with this too, you know? I just need that for me. I hope you understand. Look, call or text me, okay? We'll get breakfast again, and maybe you can meet Maddy." I shuddered at the thought of breakfast after I said it. I killed the call, started the engine, and continued forward, cranking up some heavy metal and feeling a little better.

I was going to be done with these cut ties and loose ends. I had done it with both parents. I had done it with other people in my life. I knew the knots in my stomach would lead to uncertainty and doubt in my other relationships if I didn't right all these wrongs, even if they weren't all my wrongs. It had to begin with Kenneth.

The GPS on my dashboard told me I was arriving and that the house would be on my right, but it didn't seem like it; there were no houses along the endless trees beside me. There was, however, a blue mailbox approaching, and I did eventually see the opening of a driveway. I slowed down, looking for the house within the thicket of emerald and pine and mocha, and saw nothing.

I turned onto the gravel road, entering the forest, feeling the scramble of crushed stone under the tires. It felt like the entrance to a new world, a world of stillness and seclusion. The mystery was exciting, not quite unnerving, and I considered the image of Maddy and myself living a life like this, away from it all.

The driveway made a slight curve to the left and the house revealed itself to me. It was a simple but beautiful brick building of various browns, its shutters teal and its roof triangular with several points in the structure. Small and faultless, its yard well kempt with vibrant plants and flowers to both sides of the main entrance. I was impressed.

I was also right on time, and before I even had the chance to make a complete stop in front of the one-car garage, I saw a man walking confidently from around the back of the house towards me. He had either heard the car rolling through the gravel or he was watching intently in secret anticipation.

Kenneth. It had to be. Why wouldn't it be? He was tall and positive, with the most approachable smile for a stranger. It was a little infectious. I smiled back.

I parked and got out of the car, and walked toward him, and before I could put my keys in the pocket of my jeans, he was already extending a hand for me to shake.

"Tyler," he said. The same voice as on the phone. "So good to see you, man. It's a pleasure. I'm so grateful you're here."

I shook his hand. A firm grip. "Hey, Ken."

There was something about him, something unthreatening and bookish. Maybe it was the dark gray cardigan at the end of June, the plain white polo underneath with both buttons fastened, his khaki pants, his belt and shoes the same shade of reddish pecan. Silver, flowing hair. Wide-rimmed glasses with transparent frames. Clean-shaven face. A good-looking man, I had to admit. Probably in his late fifties. Mom had done well for herself. He was clearly educated and successful, as well groomed as his yard, and cleaner and more proper than my father ever was. She had gone for the opposite man. My guess was that he was a professor. Maybe a dentist. Chiropractor? I pictured him golfing or playing tennis with his patients, talking pretentious things.

"Did you find the place okay?" he asked. "We're kind of hiding back here, huh?"

I faked a chuckle. "It's beautiful. Really nice spot back here."

"It's so great to meet you. Donna's said so much about you. Man, you really have her eyes. It's uncanny." He stared into me and I welcomed it. I was not as troubled as I would've been with anyone else I'd just met.

"I heard that a bunch growing up," I said. "That and her nose. I have her nose."

He took in a deep breath and exhaled, perhaps relieved or moved by our meeting. "Wow, I have a son. Is that awkward to say? I have a stepson."

I gave a genuine chuckle this time. "It's not awkward at all. I get it. This is all very sudden. But I guess you already knew about me, whereas for me this is all new."

"Right."

"How long did you know... about me?"

He considered the question thoughtfully. "The whole time, honestly. It just never seemed... real. You were this unknown thing that never seemed tangible, you know? Just kind of floating out there somewhere."

"Yeah." I had known similar feelings, wondering about my mom somewhere in the world, if she was even alive, and about my father when I went long periods without speaking to him.

Kenneth smiled again, his face transitioning to a happier subject. "Tell me about yourself, man. What are you up to? What's your story? What do you do for a living?"

"Oh, well, I'm a freelance writer. A blogger, basically. I write reviews for companies, trying out their products. It pays whatever. I like doing it. My fiancée is a fitness instructor with her own business. She has a studio in our town and that's how we met. She wants to open two more locations. She brings home the longest strips of bacon, which is fine by me."

He laughed. "Wow, that's fantastic. So you're engaged. That's exciting. When's the wedding?"

"October. So we've got about three and a half months. Not quite crunch time yet, but it's going to be small. Just a tiny ceremony with about six people. She has a friend performing it. I hate being the center of attention, and we want to save money, you know?"

Kenneth nodded in approval. "Absolutely. Any kids on the horizon? Step-grandchildren? I'm sorry, that was inappropriate, wasn't it? This is all so weird. I have no clue how to navigate any of this."

The question was certainly irregular, but I wasn't about to agree with him and cause tension right off the bat. "It's okay. No kids any time soon, if ever. She's very focused on her business and she's doing a phenomenal job. She's so driven and I don't know what she's doing with me."

"Nah, don't cut yourself short," Kenneth said. "I'm sure Maddy sees a lot in you. Hey, listen, you didn't come here just for me. Donna is out back, sitting by the pond. She likes to watch the fish pop up now and then."

I felt my face heat up. For a brief moment I had forgotten why I'd come here. I didn't answer, dumbstruck by the reality that I would see my mother again.

Kenneth broke the silence. "Do you want a drink before we walk back there? I'm sure you're nervous. I am too. It's before noon, but to hell with it, right? Do you like whiskey?"

"I love whiskey," I said, relieved by the offer.

"Two whiskeys comin' right up. You stay right here, and we'll walk back together with some liquid courage, alright? And you can catch up with her and then I'll give you a tour of the house."

"That'd be great," I said.

"Awesome, man. I'll be right back, okay?" He walked away from me quickly, excitedly, toward the front door, leaving me standing alone in the driveway, knowing that my mother was just on the other side of the house, sitting in the backyard, waiting for me. Was she as nervous as I was? Had she also needed a drink?

I realized I left my cell phone in the car and turned around to retrieve it; I'd promised Maddy I would call or text her when I arrived — she enforced a strict, paranoid law of knowing I got anywhere safely. I opened my driver's side door and picked up my phone, and noticed the red light in the top corner blinking wildly.

Several missed calls and voicemails.

Oh Jesus, I thought. She's freaking out about me getting here okay.

But I looked at the screen in disbelief that only one missed call was from Maddy. The rest of the calls had been from my father. And all of the voicemails had been from my father, too. I scoffed. What in the hell had I said when I called him that was so outrageous? I was extending an olive branch. I told him to call me or text me, that we could get together. Nothing appalling there.

I was about to put the phone up to my ear when Kenneth came back outside with two nine-ounce glasses, each with fine, copper elixir and ice cubes sunk to the bottom. I threw my phone back on my driver's seat and shut the door.

"Newly opened bottle," Kenneth said, handing me a glass. "Aged twenty-one years."

"Holy shit," I said, impressed. "Not cheap."

"A little over nine hundred," he replied, like it was nothing. "But it's a special occasion, wouldn't you agree? Cheers, Tyler."

He extended his glass and I clinked it with mine. I took a sip. "Amazing," I said. Rich. Dignified. "That reminds me, I told you what I did for a living. What do you do?"

He reached out his free arm to put around my shoulder, guiding me to walk with him towards the backyard. I accepted.

"I'm actually a psychiatrist. It's how I met Donna. Now, I know that probably sounds bizarre, that she was my patient, and I'll admit it wasn't something either of us planned, but in the course of helping her, we just fell in love. I think she also helped me, and it was the most profound thing in my life."

I smiled as we walked and drank together. "That's good to hear. That you were able to help her. And that she actually took the initiative of seeking help."

"She's an extraordinary woman, Tyler. It's a shame you never got to see the real her when you were growing up. I suppose this'll be like... meeting her for the first time."

I took down the rest of my whiskey, unashamed, wanting to take an ice cube in my mouth and absorb it for any modicum of alcohol remaining. *Every ounce counts.* I noticed he still had over half of his drink left. I thought about the surrealness of this moment, I thought about the strangeness of my father calling so many times, the odd panic-like feeling of it. I thought about meeting Kenneth, the conversation we had, the naturalness of it, the normalcy of him and how excited he was to meet me.

And then I saw her.

Rather, I saw the back of her, sitting in a black chair. We had made a turn around the house, and she was maybe forty feet from me, wearing a giant, floppy sun hat, facing the pond. It was a beautiful pond, surrounded by big rocks with an artificial waterfall on one side. It had a concrete walkway all around, where she was sitting. As we got closer, I realized the black chair she was in was actually a wheelchair, and my heart sank.

That's right, I thought. She's dying. No matter how well this reunion went, no matter the outcome of today, there was no beyond, no relationship, no making up for lost time. She was dying. This was temporary. She and I were still temporary. This was the time.

My mind sprinted as I looked at the back of her, her head swaying slightly in her big hat, wondering what we would say to each other, who would speak first, and I thought of everything else today — and then something hit me, an epiphany at the weirdest possible moment.

I stopped walking. Kenneth looked at me quizzically and stopped as well.

"Maddy," I said, hoarse.

"Excuse me?" Kenneth said innocently.

"My fiancée, Maddy. Her name is Madelyn."

"Yes?"

"I never told you that."

"What?"

My heart was racing now. "I never said 'Maddy' or 'Madelyn' once. You told me I was cutting myself short, that Maddy must see a lot in me."

Kenneth shrugged, not flustered in the least. He smiled. "I'm certain you told me."

"No," I insisted. I looked again at the back of my mother sitting in the wheelchair. "What's going on here? What is this?"

I started walking towards her again, quickly this time, then looked over my shoulder and noticed Kenneth was standing still, glass in hand, raising it to take a sip, calm and unaffected.

I approached her, maybe five feet behind her, and took a few breaths.

Then: "Mom?"

She didn't respond, but I noticed her head tilt under her hat like she clearly heard me. Like a confused dog.

I began walking slowly around her, taking in the moment of looking into her eyes for the first time in years, my whiskey glass still in my hand.

When I came face to face with her, I dropped the glass. It shattered on the concrete walkway surrounding the pond, startling me.

What was sitting in the wheelchair in front of me was the idea of a human being, only incomplete, like someone had begun drawing a person and never finished. After gasping and recovering from the sound of shattered glass, I stood there motionless, speechless, wondering how this was possible.

She was in a short sundress, white with yellow and orange flowers, and that was where any hint of her stopped. She had no arms, no legs, and I could tell she had no hair under her sun hat. She was a torso propped up on the wheelchair seat, fastened to it by two leather straps secured around her.

I didn't want to look into her eyes. I simply looked at the dress. It was the only piece of evidence that she was even a woman. Her large breasts that I remembered from childhood were gone, the bosom that fed me as a baby now missing. When I finally mustered the strength to look at her face, my heart skipped again and I thought I was going to pass out. She had no eyelids. Her stare was constant and wide and red with dryness, like her eyes had been in permanent shock. She was without a nose, only a black hole for a nostril like that of some alien. No ears, just two openings below her temples. She had no lips, teeth completely exposed, a snarling dog, but calm; no growl.

I met her eyes with mine and it took only a fraction of a second to know she was my mother. Everything else I remembered was long gone.

I couldn't say a word. I wouldn't have known she was even alive if it weren't for the subtle movements of her head and her chest rising and falling with air.

Kenneth approached us. "Isn't she beautiful?" he said. He pulled something tiny out of his front pocket. A bottle of eyedrops. He tilted her head back and her hat fell off as he administered the drops, confirming that she was completely bald. "I have to give them to her throughout the day — something I hadn't considered before, but it is what it is."

"What — what the fuck is this?" I said, tears now filling my eyes.

"I have a small confession to make," Kenneth said. "She never had cancer. Maybe figuratively, before I came along. You see, Tyler, your mother was in a state of depression not because she thought she was too large or too unpretty, but because she wanted to become more, to *be* more. And now she is closer than ever. She's sixty-three pounds now. She's a work of art. But not quite a masterpiece yet."

"You did this to her?" I asked.

"She asked me to. It's how we fell in love."

"Who the hell are you?" I suddenly remembered the back-alley doctors I had told Maddy about the day before, the unlicensed surgeons my father had threatened to kill over the phone. Kenneth had to have been one of them. Not a psychiatrist at all. A butcher.

"I didn't lie about one important part," Kenneth said. "This is, in fact, the last time she's going to see you. I'll be removing her eyes next. And then she'll be even closer to her oasis. Death is not an option. I want to make that very clear. I'm not a murderer, Tyler. I'm saving her. I'm making her whole. Addition by subtraction."

I looked at my mother again and searched for some semblance of a plea for help, some morsel of fear that this wasn't what she wanted. I saw nothing. Just this unfinished being, closer to a skeleton than a woman, her head practically just a skull if not for her eyes and her thin layer of flesh for a face.

"I'm calling the police," I said to Kenneth, disgusted and frightened. "This is fucking insane."

Kenneth smiled a simple smile, the same welcoming one I saw when pulling into the driveway. "I'm afraid that's not possible. You'll be staying here. I think you might need similar counseling as your mother."

That was a threat, and that was my cue to go to my car. This went from bizarre to now my life possibly being in serious danger. I walked around my mother and past Kenneth and began moving quickly back to the driveway. My phone was in my car and there was no way in hell Kenneth was going to stop me from using it.

It hit me, just then. My father. His missed calls and voicemails. He must've found out. He said he was going to look into Kenneth or have others at the station do some digging. Maybe he realized what was going on here before I did. That gave me some comfort. If anything serious was going to happen to me, there would be enough information to either find me or find this place. I was a cop's son. I knew there was no way he'd get away with whatever he was going to attempt to do to me.

I was approaching my car when I heard Kenneth yell from the pond, "Tyler! I need to talk to you, son!"

I opened the driver's door and didn't see my cell phone where I had left it.

He had it. He fucking had it.

I turned around to watch him walking towards me, and I suddenly felt very light-headed and confused. There were two of him. There were three of him. I raised my right hand to look at it and it was moving in dizzyingly slow motion, multiple hands painting through time.

The whiskey.

Every ounce counts.

"You son... of a bitch," I said to him.

I fell to my knees slowly. The earth felt like a cloud.

"Everything's going to be alright," Kenneth said. "I promise, Tyler."

I fell to my back and saw him hovering over me in a haze. I wanted to scream but the only sounds I could form were whispers. "Heh. *Hell.* Help."

Kenneth leaned down and put a hand on my forehead, then ran it calmly through my hair. "I *am* helping you." Then he used his hand to close my eyelids. The world was gone. I was gone. Floating, weightless.

SECTION FIVE

The first thought that entered my mind when I came to was that my mouth was dry and I needed water. I hadn't opened my eyes yet, but the air smelled old and stuffy, and I could taste dust in my throat. I had apparently slept with my mouth wide open. I couldn't feel much; whatever he had mixed into the whiskey had not worn off yet. Or maybe he had given me something else.

He. Kenneth. If that was his name. Soon the memory of everything that happened had finally come into focus like my brain adjusting a lens, and I could feel more of my body, the rotted wings flapping in the cage of my center. I coughed and it hurt my chest like pneumonia. It was mostly my chest that felt anything.

I opened my eyes and thankfully there was not much light. Not much adjustment needed. A single bulb was screwed in a wooden crossbeam with a string hanging down. I was in a basement, dank and unfinished. I couldn't tell if there were other sources of light down here that hadn't been turned on yet.

I heard a door open behind me, near the ceiling, and the sound of footsteps down creaking wooden stairs. His steps were normal, matter-of-fact and calm, like he was coming down to change laundry, not to see the stepson he was holding captive.

"Tyler?" he said softly behind my shoulder. "You awake?"

I craned my neck in response and he breathed a sigh of relief. He walked around me, hovering over me, looking down at my face.

"Tyler," he said proudly. "You're doing so well. Here, I brought you some mineral water." He had a plastic bottle in his hand with the top already twisted off, and he began moving it towards my lips.

"No," I managed from my gravel throat. "I'm not drinking another thing you give me."

He smiled. "I don't blame you. But you can trust me this time. Promise. You need electrolytes and vitamins and all that good stuff. You've come a long way."

A long way. From where? When? As I was becoming more conscious of the reality around me, and I was beginning to feel more and more awake, I opened my eyes wider and looked around Kenneth and the basement we were in. I was clearly sitting down, judging by the angle he was looking at me. The basement was typical: a rough concrete floor and unpainted brick walls. The only familiar objects I could see with the limited lighting were a twin mattress in one corner, no frame or box spring, with a single pillow and ratty blanket. And there were maybe a dozen oil drums grouped in another corner. Some were rusty and clearly old, others were newer and plastic, but they were all unmistakably 55-gallon drums, maybe three feet tall. In the center of the basement was what looked like a hospital bed with a table next to it, displaying various tools that were foreign to me. Saws and knives. There were several wooden bookcases lining the walls with large tomes that had to have been textbooks — medical, I assumed.

"It's been three days," Kenneth said. "You're recovering faster than the others."

"Others?" I whispered.

"We'll get there," he said. "But for now, take a look at what we've achieved."

I had no idea what he was talking about, but I could see him looking below my chin, and down near my legs.

I slowly brought my head down to look at them, but confusion seemed to overwhelm me.

There were no legs.

I was sitting in a wheelchair, and I could tell because I saw the edge of my seat and the support pedals near the floor. Everything was an empty space beyond my pelvic area, and I couldn't tell or feel if all of that was even intact, either.

"Wha…" I said. "What the fuck did you do to me?"

He looked excited. "One limb a day. Have to take it slow. Luckily, I know what I'm doing or you would've been gone the first night. Trial and error with the others, unfortunately. We'll do the left arm tomorrow night."

The left arm. I turned my head to the left to look at my arm and was relieved to see it was still there. I turned right and the dust in my throat was replaced with bile. My other arm was gone.

Looking down at the dreck I'd made on myself, I now noticed the same types of straps holding me to the chair that were holding my mother outside.

Kenneth walked away from me and to the metal table next to the hospital bed. He picked up a dirty rag, stained with blotches of dark red, and came back to me. He began wiping the puke off my shirt and the wheelchair.

"No worries," he said, leaning down on one knee now. "It happens. Surprised it wasn't sooner." He stopped wiping and looked face-to-face with me, our eyes level. "You're a strong one, Tyler. Stronger than I ever could've guessed. Your demons have made you look frailer than you are." He stood back up, holding the plastic bottle of mineral water to my lips. "Please, drink. We have a lot to talk about."

"There's nothing," I began. "There's nothing to talk about. You're a fucking psychopath."

He made a genuine frown. "A reasonable reaction to all this, I know. The thought has crossed my mind over the years."

I heard a wriggling sound in the corner, where the barrels were. Possibly a rat, or several, down here with us. I focused my attention back to Kenneth. "Why are you doing this?"

"I'll be right back," he said, walking past me toward the stairs. "Your mother just finished lunch. She'll want to see you."

He walked upstairs, leaving me strapped to the wheelchair, staring down in disbelief at the remainder of myself, my body. I wasn't quite terrified; whatever I had been drugged with kept me numb to a lot of emotion, not just the pain.

I was alone again in the quiet darkness of the basement, unable to move or free myself. I was weak, but I knew I needed a plan. I had always wanted to be optimistic, to have hope, which was probably why I made the drive to meet Kenneth and see my mom one last time. Hope. The promise of something good on the horizon. It's why I had called my father, too. But the state I was in, the loss of blood, the feeling of dread, made hope almost unreachable.

Madelyn. Maddy. Little Dipper. I realized I might never see her again.

I could hear him walking up there differently now. Shorter, heavier steps. He was carrying something large. He approached the first step back down and I already knew what it was. He was carrying my mother down. I pictured him cradling her with her chin on his shoulder, like an infant. He reached the bottom step and walked around to me. She could've been an unfinished mannequin, bald and now naked, had it not been for her quick breathing. She was afraid. I could feel it.

He took her to the dirty mattress in the corner and laid her down on her back, just a nude torso and head on a ratty bed. He looked back at me and smiled, an unwelcome smile, not the trusting one from our first meeting. He looked back down at her, sweating, and began unzipping his pants. Her body was wiggling in protest.

"You don't want this, do you?" Kenneth said to her. My mother quietly but firmly shook her head no. "You never wanted this. Any of this. I know you didn't."

He laid down on top of her and I looked away, staring down at the emptiness where I used to be. I couldn't bear to look. I heard the unmistakable, animalistic sobs of a woman with no voice, just the guttural, sinus noise of an innocent person's throat altered and mutilated.

You never wanted this. Any of this. I know you didn't. I finally broke down into tears. She had never agreed to her current state. This had happened against her will. Maybe she was just like me. And like her, I fell for it.

I heard him finish and stand up, zip his pants back up and walk over to me. He didn't look at me, just moved past me to my right. I watched as he went to the other side of the basement that I hadn't bothered looking at yet. There was a small coffee table with a vintage record player, and a milk crate with vinyl records on the floor next to it. He bent down and leafed through the collection with his fingers, made a selection and placed it on the player.

The unmistakable crackling of needle on vinyl was followed by striking piano chords, chords too beautiful for this basement and everything in it.

Kenneth turned around and walked back to me, but he didn't stand still. He paced slowly around me as I stayed motionless in the wheelchair. He was a slow carousel of dread, away from sight on my left and returning on my right.

"Do you know this?" he asked, referring to the music.

He was now behind me.

"It's Claude Debussy. He started composing his final cycle in 1914 called *Six Sonatas for Various Instruments.*"

He was back in front of me.

"However, he had terminal cancer and was only able to complete three of them by the time he died in 1918."

Behind me.

"This is the *Cello Sonata*. Classical in the best sense of the word. Quiet and mournful."

In front of me.

"There's a sorrow here. I play it down here for my subjects. The enlightened. I know it soothes them. I see it in their eyes — well, some of their eyes."

Behind me.

"The melancholy, of still being *here*, but the fortune of knowing they're so close to their private oasis. They're emotional but still divine, like how I imagine Debussy in his final years writing this."

In front of me. This time he stopped, kneeled down, and looked into my eyes. The music continued.

"What makes you human, Tyler?"

I didn't respond.

"I mean you specifically. Was it your arms? Your legs? I can take those away and you're still a human being, right? Is it your eyes, your lips, your ears? You'd still be a person in my book."

I looked back into his eyes in silence.

"Come on, Tyler, you have to have an opinion. Not a tough question, right?"

I tried to work up saliva to spit in his face, but he knew. He saw my cheeks shifting.

"Don't even think about it, or I'll make you fuck your mother harder than I just did."

He smiled.

I swallowed.

"Come on, think," he continued.

"My soul," I whispered.

He frowned in consideration. "Interesting. Not really a tangible thing, right? How many things can I whittle away at until you're not a person anymore? Circulatory system? Just a brain and a heart? And then your soul?"

"You're trying to... reduce people to their essence. But you don't know what that is."

"Your mother came to me with a problem. Like all the others. She felt so large. She hated what she saw in the mirror. She told me the disgusting depths she went to while you and your father were still around, before you both left her, like heartless, careless bastards."

"I cared. My father cared. It was never enough. She was never skinny enough."

"Trying to become weightless. I told you what she weighs now. Sixty-three pounds. Isn't that terrific? It's not quite zero, but we're getting there."

"You can't. It doesn't work that way."

"Like I said. Trial and error."

I began sobbing. "You call them the enlightened?"

He looked over to the 55-gallon drums in the corner. One of them wiggled. Then another. "Do you know what it's like to feel weightless, Tyler? I've tried it. I never succeeded. I would lie in a tank of water, my senses cut off from the world, in total darkness, and just float without sight or smell. All my worries, my anxieties, gone for hours. I could do anything. Feel anything. Be anything. An hour could feel like a day. But I knew it wasn't real. No matter how deep I let the high of floating rush through me, I knew it wasn't right. But I was close to something."

One of the containers wiggled loudly. "SHUT UP!" Kenneth yelled, startling me.

He got up and walked over to the drums. He took a few deep breaths, trying to compose himself. Then, he removed the lid from the drum wiggling the hardest, a rancid smell immediately exiting and drifting to me.

"This is Oliver," he said. He reached into the container and pulled up a man, no arms, no legs. His head moved wildly. He had no eyes or nose. Kenneth held him up from behind to display to me. "He can't hear or speak or see. I removed his teeth and tongue. He's a feisty one, but he's one of my favorites. He tries not to give up. Isn't that funny? He thinks there's a future in the old way, but I know what he doesn't know. He's getting closer. He's closer to what he longed for, to what he came to me about in the first place."

I felt like vomiting again. Bodies. Alive. In all the drums. Twelve of them.

"I know you look at Oliver and you see something monstrous, perhaps even sad. A freak, trapped in his own piss and shit all day. But I see something beautiful. I see a soul, potentially free, in darkness. No distractions, and soon, no worries. Just life in its purest form. Soon, he won't even be Oliver anymore. He won't be anyone, or anything. He'll just... be."

"Is that what he wants?" I asked, half-believing I was about to wake from a nightmare. "Is that what any of them want?"

"I think they do. Most of them. Some of them don't know it yet. Like your mother. She acts like a person, but I'll ask you again. What makes a person? She has no favorite books anymore, no songs, no poems, no identity."

"She could still have those things. She has memories, Kenneth."

Before Kenneth could answer, we both heard a loud crash from upstairs. It sounded like a door being broken open by force. Kenneth looked at me, startled.

"POLICE!" I heard a voice shout upstairs. It was undoubtedly my father's. Then, there were other footsteps above, more voices and more movement.

Kenneth dropped Oliver back into the drum, then ran to the other side of the basement. There was a window along the brick wall, up near the ceiling, and he climbed up one of the wooden bookcases, shattered the glass window, and leapt through. Just like that. Gone.

I heard footsteps racing downstairs. "Tyler? Ty? You down here?"

He got to the bottom of the steps and raced around to me; his pistol was drawn. He looked at me in complete shock, then began to cry.

"Oh my God," he said quietly. He began loosening the straps around me.

"That way," I said, nodding toward the window. My father looked at it and then back at me. "I'm okay," I said. "I'm fine. I promise. Just go."

My father started for the steps.

Then he stopped as he saw the mattress in the corner, and what was lying on it.

"Dad, don't look. Just go," I pleaded to him.

I knew he could see her. He stood there silently, barely comprehending.

"Donna?"

"DAD! JUST GO!"

He put a hand up to his mouth, covering it, hiding his horror, then he ran back up the stairs.

I could hear him shouting at the other officers to follow him outside, in the direction I pointed. Something told me Kenneth would get away. I didn't know why I knew; I just did.

It was just me now, alone with the others. With her. The enlightened.

I looked down at myself to see how loose my father had been able to get the straps, and was excited to see that my remaining arm, my only limb, was free. I quickly unfastened the rest of the straps, and could feel myself free in the chair. I looked over at the mattress, at my mother, helpless and cold, exposed to the world.

Every ounce counts.

I had to make a decision, one that would hurt me, maybe even kill me. I scooted myself forward and used my arm to push myself off the chair, and I landed hard and awkwardly onto the concrete basement floor. I took a moment to let the pain subside, angry that there was feeling finally returning to my body.

Every ounce counts.

I used my arm with all my strength to crawl to her, slowly and painfully, sobbing with physical agony, emotional agony. My fingernails cracked and peeled as I pulled my remaining weight, sliding through five jagged trails of blood, one for each throbbing digit.

Every ounce counts.

My hand was touching soft mattress rather than hard concrete. I kept pulling until I felt flesh. I scooted up next to her, her eyes locked on mine, finally, reunited. We lay there quietly, taking in the moment, the recognition of all we'd both been through, past and present.

"I love you," I said. "I'm so sorry."

Tears were streaming down her face, her eyes red and irritated from her lack of lids to protect them.

I maneuvered myself to lay on my side, my arm above me, free to make movement. I gently placed my bloody hand around her throat, not squeezing, just holding her softly. Not squeezing. Not just yet.

"Do you want me to?" I asked her, crying.

She nodded without hesitation. She smiled, and I smiled, and I kissed her cheek.

I used whatever energy I had left to squeeze. I squeezed until she writhed, until she wiggled and jerked, until she wasn't moving anymore.

I stayed there with her, my head on her chest, listening for a heartbeat to see if I was too weak to do what she asked. There was none. I had given her peace. I had given her freedom. I had done what Kenneth could and would never do.

I heard some of the 55-gallon drums jerking again, bodies squirming and twitching in pain and panic. I looked at them, and then I looked around the basement, hoping to find something, anything, that could help them.

In one of the dark corners, just barely visible, was a portable generator for the house. I couldn't think of any use for it, but there was a small red, plastic container sitting next to it, with a long, yellow spout coming out.

Then I wondered if the basement had a lighter or a box of matches lying around.

SECTION SIX

There were months of physical therapy and counseling, but I knew I'd be okay. The worst part was that I had to learn how to type and write with just my left hand. Very slowly, I began writing more. I began writing all this. It's taken me years. All this darkness, from my childhood to that basement.

Of course, I had counted wrong in the darkness, in the chaos and my sedation. There were thirteen oil drums in the corner of the basement, not twelve. It took a few months for the forensics team and the FBI to confirm the prisoners' identities. Dental records weren't possible for half of them. Fingerprints were clearly not an option. My fear was that I had made it harder for them to test the bodies due to the fire I had started, but with the advancements in criminal science and DNA analysis, my father was able to give me a list of names. I was grateful to learn about some of them.

Meghan Price was a stay-at-home mom of three battling depression. Jonathan Krone was an alcoholic; his oldest daughter had died in a car crash. Suzanne Ryan was a stripper with a drug addiction. Oliver Roland was a prosecutor who had failed to put away a prolific child molester. Colin Hawkins was a struggling college student with a history of self-harm. Michelle Lacey developed an eating disorder after she caught her husband cheating on her. Donna Shepherd, formerly Donna Swanson, born Donna Gaines, suffered from body dysmorphia and convinced herself she was obese.

There was also Karen Lehman, and Richard Pye, and Klara Dunkle, and Lauren Basso, and Anthony Greenberg, all with their own tragedies that I never had a chance to catch up on. But the thirteenth body, housed back in the farthest of the corner in the basement, in a steel drum while most of the others were plastic, could not be identified. The fire had barely burned him. He died of smoke inhalation.

It wasn't my intention to possibly deny their families of ever finding out what happened to them. At that moment, the only objective in my mind was putting them out of their misery. Putting myself out of my own misery. If Kenneth had successfully continued with his experiments on me, and I had woken up blind and deaf and without vocal cords in a steel drum with nothing but my own thoughts, I'd want someone to kill me too. By any means necessary. My easiest option was burning the house down.

And the house was destroyed. The fire had spread above the basement quickly and there was nothing left of it within minutes. But before the inferno brought it all down, my father, ever the hero cop, dashed through the house and to the basement and got me out. I suffered minor injuries from the fire. My father had third degree burns up his right arm; he's okay now. Mostly healed. He's a tough guy. He hadn't even known it happened until we arrived at the hospital.

Kenneth Shepherd wasn't caught, as I had predicted. Just like I predicted that Kenneth Shepherd wasn't his name. It took my father some time to dig into that alias before he frantically called me that day, but the only Kenneth Shepherd that could've made sense within three states had died three years ago. The remains of the old lady who owned the house I drove to had been kept in the attic. She had no family. Nobody had a clue about her. Other results showed no marriage to a Donna Gaines or a Donna Swanson. No marriage had occurred. There was relief in knowing that I never had a stepfather in the first place.

After obsessive investigation on and off the clock, my father did find several profiles online that looked like the man I described, and eventually confirmed they were all him. He was Martin McCray, he was Martin Merak, he was Kenneth Nowak, Christopher Shepherd. He was a dozen more names in half the United States. Leonard McCray. Martin Rawson. Leonard Rawson.

There had been good news despite all this. Madelyn and I got married two years after the fire. I needed time to recover and come to terms with the man I now was, bound to a motorized chair, my left arm my only remaining limb, completely dependent on Maddy's help. It was a job she didn't deserve and I didn't want her to have, but she was just like the name of her fitness studios: Mad Strong. She continued managing her gym and eventually opened up four more, two in our county and two in another. She was able to stay home more while other managers took care of them. I continued to love her, and she continued to love me, even though the man she married was less than he was before.

On my wedding day, my father pushed me down the aisle in a wheelchair. We became closer during those two years after everything. I knew it was still killing him not being able to catch "The Back-Alley Butcher" (as he came to be called in the media), and that was why I knew the day that came recently would eventually come.

My father came over to the house while Maddy was at work, which was a regular habit for him now, only he looked different this time. He had adrenaline coursing through him. He was carrying an eight-by-ten manila envelope. He sat on the couch as I stayed in my motorized chair. He fought with himself over telling me. He kept the envelope pressed against his chest, the same damn way Maddy held The Back-Alley Butcher's letter two years ago.

"I talked to some people that I probably shouldn't have talked to," he said. "Got a tip that someone who looks exactly like him is residing in Belarus. I found him online. It's him. He's done some work on himself, but it's him."

"Europe?" I asked. I wasn't necessarily surprised; he would've been an idiot if he'd stayed in the states, and an idiot he was not.

My father nodded. "He's posting ads for the cheapest plastic surgeries in town, showing fake licenses. His name is tied to a business called Polaris Surgery Consulting. No address, of course. A couple investigators are keeping an eye on him, but the news here didn't spread much over there. This time he's using the name Carmine Merak."

I shook my head no. "Dad."

"I can get a good deal on a flight."

"Dad," I said louder.

"Be back in four days. Or not. I've got plenty of vacation time. You know I never take vacation."

I exhaled. "I think you need to let this go."

"Why?"

"Because I have."

"I'm gonna fucking kill him."

"Don't. Someone will get him, okay? It's not worth it. We need peace. Have peace with this. I'm okay. Okay?"

My father got choked up but tried to fight it. "I let him get away," he replied with a struggle.

"You *told* me not to go there," I said. "You told me. You called me and I didn't answer. Maddy told me I didn't have to go. I had to pull over to throw up when I was driving there. I knew something wasn't right. My body knew it. She knew it. She knew it the moment she took that letter out of the mailbox. Okay? This is not your fault at all."

He nodded, weeping now.

"Hey," I said. "Look at me."

He looked up, his eyes filled with tears.

"This was *my* decision," I said. "This was me. And I'm okay with it. We have a lot of choices in this life and I made one."

He considered what I said, then stared at the manila envelope in his hands. "Well, you have to make another one." He reached out with the envelope in his hand, but I hesitated in taking it.

"Whatever it is, I don't need to know," I said.

"It's not about him," he said. "It's about something else."

I took the envelope, not understanding what he meant.

My father got up and walked towards the front door. "Open it," he said with his back to me. "Or don't. Up to you. But I love you, son. Always have. I hope you know that."

He left, and I sat there in silence, not knowing what to do with the eight-by-ten manila envelope in my lap. What I did know, however, was that I was content. That anxiety? That rot in my stomach? It was gone. I felt the weight of the world off my shoulders. I might have been physically lighter, but I was emotionally lighter, too. I used to feel like I weighed more than my body, like I was five-hundred pounds inexplicably hidden in my two-hundred-pound body.

And that's when I started to understand. It began to click. My mother felt like she was five-hundred pounds. I don't know why she did, I don't know what happened in her life to make her that way; maybe nothing happened at all. I suspect something did, because she had failed to do what I did for her in that cold basement, and what I later achieved: letting go.

Letting go of her, of my animosity towards my father, of "Kenneth Shepherd" and what he did to me and my mother, and that dread. I dissevered it from my life.

Maybe it sounds vile, but The Back-Alley Butcher actually helped me. And I began wondering if his subjects, his "enlightened," felt they were being helped, too. It did bother me not knowing.

Time went by, maybe a year. It had cost more than twelve-thousand dollars, but Maddy and I had a sensory deprivation tank installed in our spare bedroom. It was a large, white vault, eight feet long and four feet wide, with room temperature water pumped inside. It was difficult getting in and out on my own, my left arm my only way to occupy it. I was the only one who used it regularly. She tried it once, but got out within a few minutes. She didn't like it. She said it felt claustrophobic, physically and mentally. She said she didn't like being trapped in her own thoughts. I told her the point was to become one with your inner self and find your soul. She said that's what exercise was for. I told her it *was* exercise, for the soul. She didn't get it. I couldn't understand why she didn't get it.

I became obsessed with the tank. I floated in there for hours, and eventually it was large portions of the day. I reached weightlessness. I was weightless, in the dark and silent. Hours felt like minutes, minutes felt like hours. I was just a soul, floating beyond the limits of a fragile vessel of blood and flesh. I didn't need any limbs. I didn't need my eyes or my nose or my hair, and I began wondering: what makes me a person?

The relentless onslaught of television and internet and talking and driving and worrying and arguing and politicizing. Gone. It was simply gone. I was a baby, back in the womb, back inside my mother, naked and unaware of the world. Floating, weightless.

But something was still wrong. I felt weightless most of the time, but there was something in the darkness sneaking in its way in, that ruined my last session in the float tank.

That damn manila envelope.

I was able to keep it hidden under our bed for twelve long months without thinking about it, but that feeling of letting go, of being at peace, just wasn't absolute enough. It would always be there, under that bed, and if I had burned it, ripped it, thrown it away, buried it, it would still keep my soul at bay from freedom.

A week had gone by since I'd seen my father, and I started to worry. He hadn't come over like he usually had. I figured he was busy with work, or he was becoming more comfortable with me by myself, or he didn't find it necessary to sit in boredom anymore while I floated in the tank the entire time without being able to talk to him. But the speculation didn't last long when

I received a postcard in the mail. I didn't tell Maddy about it; she was working more and more, hardly home as much as in the beginning.

It was your standard four-by-six postcard, ultra-thick matte with a beautiful, colorful city at night. Written over the skyline in big fancy letters, GREETINGS FROM MINSK, BELARUS. I turned it over, not expecting a return address, and to the left of my own address were four simple words, ten characters, no word more than three letters. I ran the fingers of my left hand over them, crying, tears getting on the ink, Sergeant Detective Raymond Swanson's already-near-unintelligible writing now wet and smeared.

I got him, son.

I decided to pull the manila envelope out from under our bed. I needed to. I told my father I didn't care, but part of my whole transformation, if it meant a damn, was closing every last chapter. This was my last chapter.

At first, I didn't have a reaction when I saw what was inside. There was a peculiarity to it all, an almost scientific curiosity of what makes us human beings. I felt myself breaking down the parts needed, the essential components that still made us people. I was looking for a soul inside that envelope. There was one, but it was hurting. It was crying out in agony. It wasn't happy. It wasn't free. It just thought it was.

Maddy came home later that night to find me sitting in the dark, quiet. I had become sensitive to lights. She dropped her work bag in the hallway, put her keys on the accent table, and came in looking for me, confused in the darkness. I had always left the lights on for her while I was in the float tank.

"Tyler? Babe, are you here?" she called out.

She was startled when she saw me in the living room, sitting in my motorized chair, peaceful, waiting. I had *Cello Sonata* playing on our record player.

"Hey Big Dipper," she said.

"Hey," I replied.

"Hey, what's up? Why are you sitting in the dark? What's that music playing? Why aren't you in the tank?"

"Fell asleep here. I know, it's weird. I hate this chair."

She smiled, but I could tell she was still confused. "Sorry I'm late. Two new people signed up for classes before I could close up."

I didn't reply.

"You're awfully quiet. Did you warm up dinner for yourself?"

Finally, I spoke. "Madelyn."

"Madelyn?" she said. "Whoa, okay, something's wrong."

"My father," I said.

"Oh my god. Tyler. Is he okay?" She came rushing over to the couch next to my chair and put her hands on my remaining hand. Then she turned on the end table lamp. I squinted, the bulb like a sun.

"I know," I said.

"What? Know what?" Her concern for me was as real as it had ever been. There was nothing false about it.

I pointed to the coffee table in front of her. There were pictures lying on it, turned over so only their white backs showed. She looked at them quizzically, then began flipping them.

She stared at them, taking them in, in disbelief. "Jesus Christ," she said. She buried her face in her hands and just sat there.

I could tell she knew my father had taken most of them. Some were grainy cell phone pictures; others were crystal clear, black and white, as if captured by a pro. A private eye, maybe. Others were clearly taken by him, notes and dates and times written sloppily in red pen in the white spaces.

They showed her with a man. He was fit and tall. He had muscles and he had smiles and he had limbs. He had his limbs all over her. All four of them. Some pictures were inside the gym, some were outside, some were in a car, and others were peeping through the bedroom window of an apartment.

"Tyler, I was going to tell you." She said this quietly after an eternity of silence.

"I highly doubt that," I said.

"I've been through a lot, too. I know I didn't go through what you went through, but this has been a hard time for me."

"I know."

She looked into my eyes. "You do?"

"I've asked a lot of you," I said. "You didn't have to stick around. But you did."

"Tyler, I'm 'sticking around' because I love you."

"Then why did you do this?" I nodded to the pictures.

"Because I haven't felt alive," she said. "I haven't felt awake. I'm just numb and dreaming. I'm not happy at work. I'm just going through the motions now. Floating. And when Marcus joined the studio..."

"Marcus?" I interrupted.

"Yeah. He doesn't know about you. He's a good guy. He's a really good guy. He wouldn't be doing this if he knew. This is all my fault, Tyler. He's done nothing wrong."

"You don't feel alive?" I asked.

"I... No."

"I feel more alive now than I ever have in my life, and look at me," I said.

"I know you've made peace. With everything. You know how proud I am of you."

"How can I have found peace and you haven't?"

"I don't know," she replied.

"You feel like you're my mother now."

"What?" She was shocked by that statement, maybe because of how true it was.

"I'm your child that you have to take care of. Your burden."

"Tyler, that's not true," she said.

"You won't even touch me."

"That has nothing to do with..."

"You look at me different. Like something else. Less than. Below you."

"I do not."

"Just say it," I said, shaking my head.

"I don't know what I feel," she said. "But it's not that."

She got off the couch and got closer to me. She got down on her knees in front of me and placed my hand on her cheek, holding it tightly, my hand wet from her tears.

"I won't talk to him anymore. He's gone."

"Madelyn."

She began crying. "I'll ban him from the studio. Sever all ties with him."

"It's not about that," I said, shaking my head.

"Then what do I have to do, Tyler? Huh? I'll do anything. I love you. I do. Just tell me. I'll do anything you tell me. I can't do this anymore."

She followed me into the kitchen, and into the garage. I tried to comfort her as I told her what to grab. She was confused and scared. Then she followed me into the bedroom and she displayed the items on the bed. And then she understood. She saw it clearly. The crosscut hand saw. The fretsaw. The steak knife. The pliers. We climbed onto the bed, naked, and I guided her.

"Big Dipper," I whispered into her ear, and I patted my chest with my hand.

She looked at me, crying with love and anticipation, and then she smiled.

"Little Dipper," she said, shaking. Then she patted her own chest with her hand.

She made the first cuts herself, with her legs, her blood pouring and spraying on the bed, on me. She needed my help in holding her right arm down. She was getting weak. We finished it together. I knew she wasn't going to make it. I knew her vessel of blood and flesh couldn't endure, but I held her, kissing her, telling her it would all be okay soon.

We cherished each other that night, embracing and swaying to the cadence of what was only love, her body fluttering and sending waves of excitement through my own, better forces flying around the cage of my center. I felt at home and free from harm, and it didn't matter anymore what happened. I was invincible with her devotion, and as we lay in bed later in our calm euphoria, she stared into my eyes with affection and we fell asleep, floating, weightless.

Z.C. Krol lives in Ohio with his wife and dogs, and is working on another project. When he's not writing, he's probably watching a bad horror movie or reading something creepy. You can email him at zckrol.writing@gmail.com and he'll absolutely respond to you. You can also find him on this new website called Facebook. Bonus points if you send him horror memes.

www.ingramcontent.com/pod-product-compliance
Lightning Source LLC
Chambersburg PA
CBHW031427130726
47989CB00003B/1056